KT-158-932

013754990 5

This
BOOK
belongs to .oooooooooooooooooooo

First published in 2010 by Child's Play (International) Ltd
Ashworth Road, Bridgemead, Swindon SN5 7YD

Distributed in USA by Child's Play Inc
250 Minot Avenue, Auburn, Maine 04210

Distributed in Australia by Child's Play Australia Pty Ltd
Unit 10/20 Narabang Way
Belrose, NSW 2085

ISBN 978-1-84643-344-3
HH120110PB04103443

Printed and bound in Heshan, China

1 3 5 7 9 10 8 6 4 2

A catalogue record of this book is available from the British Library

www.childs-play.com

Star Gazers, Sky Scrapers & extraordinary Sausages

by Claudia Boldt

Careful, Frank!
Don't knock my ice-cream!

I'd love to make ice-creams
when I grow up. What about you?

I am going to be a sausage dog!
I want to make sausages,
eat sausages, do sausages.
Sausages, Sausages,
Sausages!

Oh, Frank!
That's so boring!

When I grow up, I will be climbing the steepest skyscrapers, up amongst the ice-cream clouds.

Sausages!
Mmmm... sausages!

Or I could be a lighthouse keeper.
I could flash the light, while you guide
the ships safely out to sea!

Sau-sea-ges, splash!
Sau-sea-ges, blub!
Sau-sea-ges...

Or I might be a star gazer!
We could be astronauts
on the first mission to Mars!

Space-sa-ges!
Zoom!

Come dance with me!

I could be
a superdancer!

A leaping, zeaping,
ice-cream-eating
superdancer!

Sau-sa-ges.
Sass-se-ges.
Siss-se-ges.
Sou-sa-ges.
Salsa-ges.
S-A-U-S-A-G-E-S.

I could be Queen Bee, and you could be my worker!

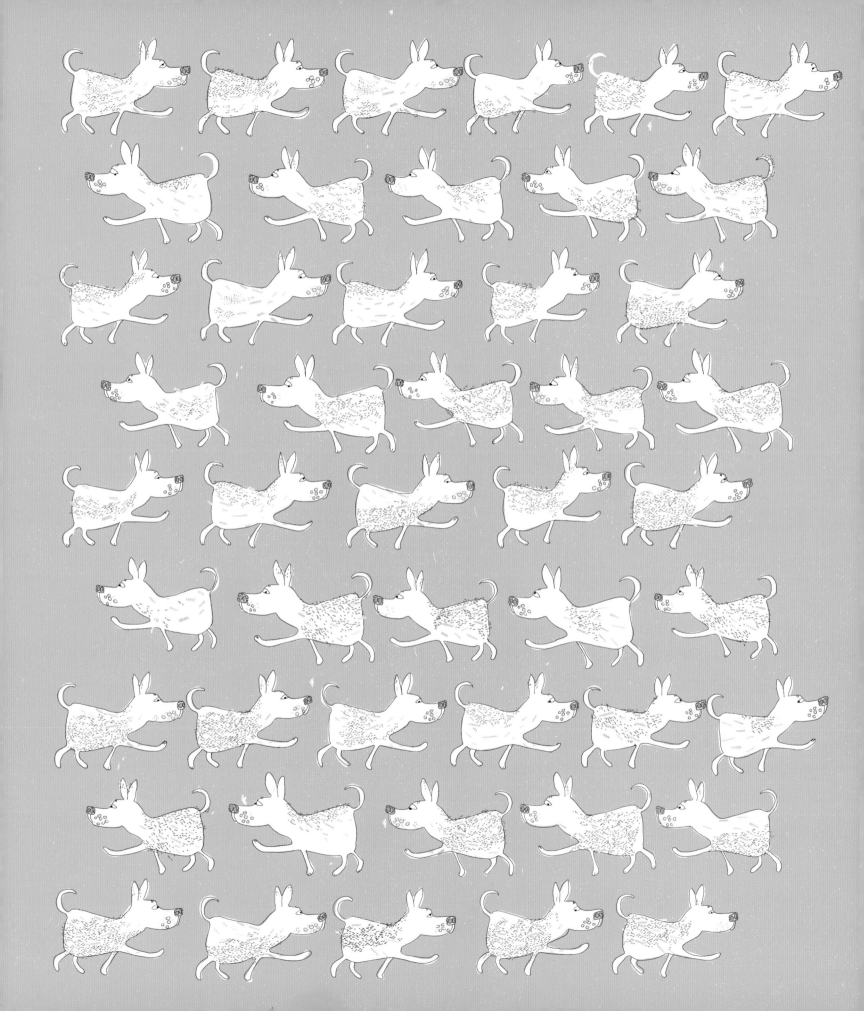

You'll love this.
I'm going to be a mechanic!

Sausages!

It's not fair!
You never want to do
anything with me!

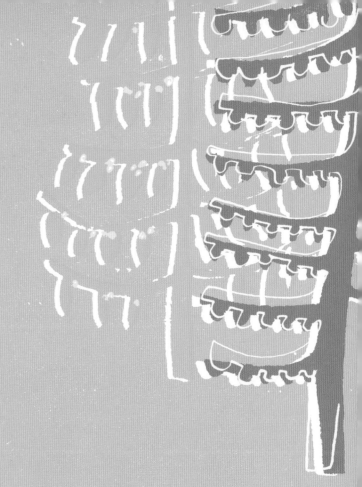

Sausages?

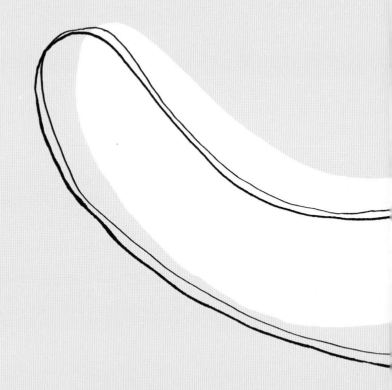

I like sausages and
sitting down! You like
ice-cream and moving around!
We have nothing
in common!

Slurp!

Chomp!

Frank?
Are you thinking
what I'm thinking?

ICE-CREAM SAUSAGES!
SAUSAGE ICE-CREAM!